Topic: Transportation and Safety **Subtopic:** Emergency Vehicles

Notes to Parents and Teachers:

The books your child reads at this level will have more ⬚ details to discuss. Have children practice reading more ⬚ Take turns reading pages with your child so you can model what fluent reading sounds like.

REMEMBER: PRAISE IS A GREAT MOTIVATOR!

Here are some praise points for beginning readers:

- I love how you read that sentence so it sounded just like you were talking.
- Great job reading that sentence like a question!
- WOW! You read that page with such good expression!

Book Ends for the Reader!

Here are some reminders before reading the text:

- Use your eyes to follow the words in the story instead of pointing to each word.

- Read smoothly and with expression. Read like you are talking. Reread sections of the book to practice reading fluently.

- Look for interesting illustrations and words in the story.

Words to Know Before You Read

ambulance

firefighter

fire truck

ladders

motorboat

police car

police officer

sirens

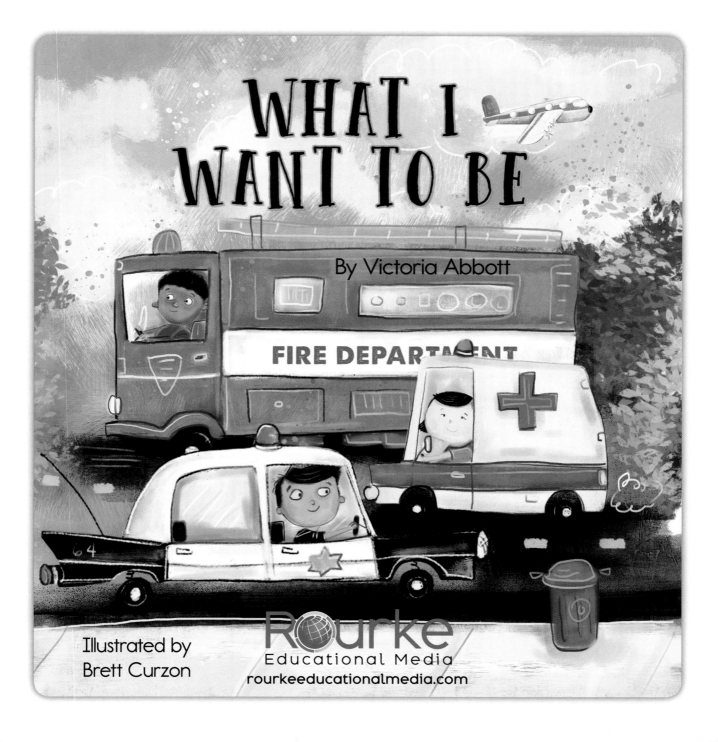

I ride on the fire truck.
I climb ladders.

I put out fires. Look, I am very brave.

FIRE DEPARTMENT

What do I want to be when I grow up?

I want to be a firefighter!

I drive an ambulance.
I turn on my sirens.

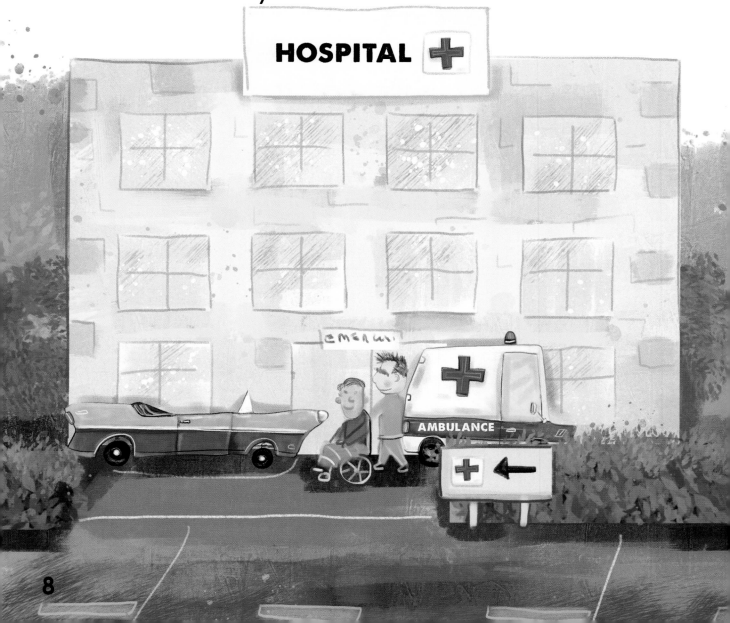

I drive to the hospital. Look, I drive very safely.

What do I want to be when I grow up?

HOORAY FOR
THE AMBULANCE DRIVERS!!!

I want to be an ambulance driver!

I drive a police car. I catch a robber.

I help people cross the road. Look, I direct the traffic.

What do I want to be when I grow up?

HOORAY FOR THE POLICE!!!

I want to be a police officer!

I drive a motorboat.
I rescue swimmers.

I dive into the ocean. Look, I swim
very fast.

What do I want to be when I grow up?

HOORAY FOR THE COAST GUARD!!!

I want to be in the Coast Guard!

We will all help people. We will all save people from danger.

That is who we want to be.

Book Ends for the Reader

I know...

1. What will you do if you become a firefighter?

2. What will you do if you become an ambulance driver?

3. What will you do if you are in the Coast Guard?

I think ...

1. Have you ever seen firefighters? What were they doing?

2. Have you ever seen an ambulance?

3. What do you want to be when you grow up? Why?

Book Ends for the Reader

What happened in this book?

Look at each picture and talk about what happened in the story.

About the Author

Victoria Abbott lives in Boston, Massachusetts. She has authored numerous books for children on just about every topic you can think of. An avid athlete, she has run the famous Boston marathon and when she isn't running, she enjoys paddle boarding and staying active. Whether on land or water, she is always moving!

About the Illustrator

Born in Sydney Australia, Brett Curzon now lives in northern NSW Australia with his family, his wife, three kids, two dogs and one evil cat. Brett Curzon's whimsical art can be seen in children's books to drink bottles. If not working away, he can be found in the ocean, or at the very least only a few feet away.

Library of Congress PCN Data

What I Want to Be / Victoria Abbott

ISBN 978-1-68342-741-4 (hard cover)(alk. paper)
ISBN 978-1-68342-793-3 (soft cover)
ISBN 978-1-68342-845-9 (e-Book)
Library of Congress Control Number: 2017935456

Rourke Educational Media
Printed in the United States of America, North Mankato, Minnesota

www.rourkeeducationalmedia.com

Edited by: Debra Ankiel
Art direction and layout by: Rhea Magaro-Wallace
Cover and interior Illustrations by: Brett Curzon